damsel

damsel

S.E. CONNOLLY

ILLUSTRATED BY
AXEL RATOR

MERCIER PRESS
IRISH PUBLISHER – IRISH STORY

MERCIER PRESS

Cork

www.mercierpress.ie

Trade enquiries to CMD,
55A Spruce Avenue, Stillorgan Industrial Park,
Blackrock, County Dublin

© Susan E. Connolly, 2009

© Illustrations: Axel Rator, 2009

ISBN: 978 1 85635 618 3

10 9 8 7 6 5 4 3 2 1

A CIP record for this title is available from the British Library

 Mercier Press receives financial assistance from the
Arts Council/An Chomhairle Ealaíon

Printed and bound in the EU.

To my friends and family.
I have more and better of both
than anyone could ever hope for.

chapter 1

The messenger wore very fine boots. They were made of black leather with gold embroidery, only a little dusty from the road. Annie studied the boots while he talked, trying to block out the meaning behind his words. She only looked away when her mother collapsed into his arms. Annie wondered if she should collapse into someone's arms as well, but the messenger's were full of her mother, and her brother Joffrey was only a baby and she didn't think he'd like to be squashed. So instead she made some tea, saw the messenger out the door and put her mother to bed.

She sat in front of the fire, studying the flames

and listening to her mother's sobs from upstairs while she tried to figure out what she should do.

Father had been gone a very long time. After Joffrey had been born he'd promised mother that he wouldn't go away again, that he'd give up the heroing life and stay at home to finish his book. Then the news had come that the wizard Greenlott was terrorising the kingdom, and before you could say 'death-defying peril' he was off questing again. The wizard's evil, a dragon on the rampage and the ever-present threat from the Prince Frog, meant that there were no heroes available for a rescue.

Annie wasn't a hero. She was ten years old and had long blonde hair and blue eyes, and her father said she'd make an excellent damsel one day. He had her practising her screams every morning for an hour and said they were the best he had ever heard. But now her father was missing and there were no heroes available, and her mother wouldn't stop crying.

Annie started pacing back and forth on the stone floor.

'I know I'm not a hero,' she thought to herself, 'but I've heard all father's stories, and surely even a going-to-be damsel is better than nothing? Besides, if I take the book, it will be almost as if father himself is going on the quest.'

She hadn't really convinced herself, so she sat in her father's chair in his study and opened up the book. It was a large book with brown leather covers and gold twirly bits around the edges, and on the front and down the spine in raised gold letters it said:

how to slay dragons
- and other advice for the hero in training.

The first page inside had a dedication where her father thanked his family. It said:

To my darling wife, my wonderful son,
and my beautiful daughter, who will be an
astounding damsel one day.

The next page held a single line of script:

A hero is a man who continues to try, even when all hope seems gone.

Annie looked down the contents until she found the entry that said **questing** and turned to that page.

Before you set out on your quest, you must know where you are going and what you are doing. Decide if you are going on a Rescue Quest, a Slaying Quest, or a Treasure Quest.

Annie took out her pencil and put a tick beside **rescue quest.**

For a Rescue Quest you must first decide who you are rescuing. Is it a princess, a kingdom, a damsel, a baby, a magic jewel, or other?

Annie drew an arrow up from 'other', and then wrote 'Father'.

Then you must know what you are rescuing them from. Is it a troll, a giant, an ogre, a witch, a dragon, a wizard, or other?

Annie put a tick beside 'wizard'.

Finally, you must know where to go to rescue them.

Annie chewed the back of her pencil for a while and looked around the room. She knew Greenlott's castle was at the peak of the Mountain of Misery, but she didn't know where that was or how to get there. Then she saw a drawer in her father's desk marked 'maps'. She rooted through it for a while, and found a map that showed both her house and the Mountain of Misery. It was marked with a note in curved script warning 'Here be dragons!' She took her pencil and put a circle around the mountain then went back to the book and skipped over the parts for slaying quests and treasure quests.

Congratulations! Now you know all about your quest. No matter what kind of quest you are going on, you will need to be prepared. As well as the usual things anyone would need for a long journey, a hero will require the following:

item 1. A Fiery Steed (for transport)

item 2. A Squire (for aid, distracting enemies, and recording your mighty deeds)

item 3. An Enchanted Sword (for slaying)

item 4. Mighty Armour (for shining. Dragon scales are best, but Basilisk hide will also do)

item 5. A Cloak (for sleeping in, and to billow heroically from shoulders)

item 6. Bandages (for heroic wounds)

item 7. Hearty Rations (for sustenance)

This was not as simple as the first part had been. Annie did not have a fiery steed. She had her pony, Chestnut, and she supposed that she could

tie some kind of portable campfire to him, but she didn't think he'd like that. He would have to do as he was, so she crossed out the 'Fiery' part and put a tick beside **item 1**. The Squire would be easy enough. Annie put her fingers to her mouth and whistled, and a big black dog came bouncing into the room.

'Good boy, Squire,' she said, 'now sit!'

Squire sat. He probably couldn't record her mighty deeds, or if he did, they'd be in dog-speak, but he'd be very good at aiding her and distracting enemies, so she put a tick beside **item 2**.

She fetched a bag from her room and put in her sleeping bag (**item 5** – she didn't particularly care about billowing, and a sleeping bag is much more comfortable than a cloak) and the first aid box (**item 6**). There were no hearts in the cupboards, but there was some tongue, so she wrapped that up and put it in the bag along with some bread, cheese, sausages and a big water bottle. That would do for **item 7**. She certainly didn't have a sword, let alone an Enchanted Sword, so she got the poker from the fire instead. For **item 4** she got her big warm coat with sequins on it and a cosy hat, because although it was still warm outside it was autumn, and it might get cold.

All the items were now ticked off.

Now it is time to start on your quest! Good luck!

Annie closed the book and fetched her usual camping equipment – steel and flint for starting fires, a little pot for cooking, plates and other useful things. She wrote a note to her mother and left it on the kitchen table. Then she put the map and the book in the bag, whistled for Squire, saddled up Chestnut and set off north.

Unfortunately, it was a windy day and Annie forgot to close the back door. If anyone had been able to read the note before it blew away, they would have seen this:

Dear Mother,

I have gone to rescue Father from the wizard. I have taken Chestnut and Squire and borrowed Father's book. I know I'm not a hero, but there is nobody else to go.

Love,
Angelina Cerestina Tiffenemina Brave.
(Annie)

chapter 2

according to the map the Mountain of Misery was much farther than Annie had ever been before. She had to pass through forests, over rivers, up hills and through Frog Country, so she was determined not to waste any time.

The road north was wide and smooth, with the river on one side and the forest on the other. It was a quiet road at the best of times, and with the danger of an encounter with the wizard and a dragon on the rampage, no one was travelling unless they had to, so Annie was not surprised when she did not meet any other travellers.

After a few hours they stopped at a grassy

clearing that led down to the river. Annie let Chestnut graze on the grass for his lunch and unpacked some bread and sausage for her own. Squire bounded into the forest and came back with a rabbit which he proceeded to eat.

After lunch, Annie filled up her water bottle from the river and they set off again. Soon the road split away from the river and there was forest on both sides. After a short while they came to a bridge over a small stream. It was quite a messy bridge, with a cluster of broken branches on the left beside a pile of round stones, and the water there shone very oddly. Annie stopped a safe distance away from it and took out the book. She was certain she had seen an entry about bridges:

Beware of Bridges

Bridges are a favourite home of trolls. Should you encounter a troll-bridge, gather a troll-hunting party. Arm them with stout sticks and swords and have them hide close to the bridge. Then send an expendable person or criminal

to cross the bridge as a decoy. The troll will come out from his home under the bridge to demand payment to cross or to eat the decoy. In fact they will probably eat them even if they pay, so we do not know why they bother to ask.

While the troll is distracted by the decoy, the troll-hunting party should come out from hiding and give it a good thrashing, then cut off its head and stick it on a pole for decoration.

A major problem of dealing with trolls is finding a suitable decoy, as they almost always get eaten up before the troll-hunting party gets there and cannot be recycled.

'Well,' thought Annie, 'that's all very well if you have both an expendable person and a troll-hunting party, but I have neither. Hopefully this bridge doesn't have a troll.'

She looked at the bridge more closely and saw that what she had thought were broken branches were actually broken bones. The mound of round objects was made of skulls, not stones and some of

the shine from stream was coming from discarded and twisted armour.

'There probably is a troll,' thought Annie, 'but best to be sure.'

'Hey!' she shouted, 'is there a troll under that bridge?'

'No,' said the troll.

'Oh good,' said Annie, though she knew very well he was lying, 'I'd feel really sorry for any troll living under this bridge.'

'Why?' said the troll suspiciously, and now Annie could see his shadow on the bank of the left side of the bridge. It was a large shadow, with many lumps and bumps that were probably being cast by a fearsome club.

'Well,' said Annie, 'there is a troll-hunting party hiding in the forest, and they've sent me as a decoy. If I don't get across the bridge safely, then they will know that there's a troll here, and they'll come and thrash it with sticks and cut off its head and stick it on a pole.'

'Then it's lucky for both of us that there's no troll,' said the troll, and Annie heard the splashing of his feet as his shadow disappeared and he moved back under the bridge.

Annie crossed the bridge as fast as she could and kept one hand on the poker just in case. Fortunately, the troll did not come out, but she still waited until she was several minutes away before she let her guard down. Then she heard the screams.

chapter 3

hey were faint screams, coming from deep in the woods.

'Help!' said the voice, 'somebody help!'

The mysterious screamer sounded desperate, but not in pain. Annie wasn't sure what to do. Every minute she wasted not rescuing her father was another minute when the wizard could kill him. But she wouldn't have been very happy if she'd been screaming for help and nobody came. Perhaps the book had something to say.

She didn't find anything under **quests** or **rescue**, or even under **random screaming**, but none of her father's stories had a hero who ignored cries for help. With Squire at her side she ventured cautiously into the forest. As the trees grew thicker and the branches lower, she dismounted from Chestnut and led him by the reins.

The forest would normally have been a peaceful place. It had tall trees, with green leaves mixed with those starting to turn red before they began to fall in winter. A thick carpet of leaves that had already fallen on top of the rich earth, muffled their footsteps. Patches of sunlight dappled the ground and illuminated small clearings where trees had fallen and new saplings had not yet grown in their place. All in all, Annie could have seen herself enjoying a nice picnic here, or perhaps a peaceful camping trip.

With the screams for help it felt sinister instead. Each rustle in the leaves made Annie jump. Every few minutes she looked behind her nervously, and she kept a tight grip on the poker in her bag with one hand, and on Chestnut's reins with the other.

As they came closer to where the screams were coming from, the way became more difficult. At

one point Annie had to duck Chestnut's head under a half fallen tree, before sliding down a tall bank of earth.

Eventually, she pushed through a thicket of dense bushes into a clearing in the forest and saw who had been screaming for help.

It was a large clearing about fifty feet wide and Annie thought it was too large to be entirely natural. The earth was scuffed and free of the saplings that should have been growing up towards the light. Most unusually, there was thick white webbing between two trees on the far side of the clearing. It extended across the entire space and high up into the trees. The web resembled a giant wheel, with spokes coming off the trees and meeting in the middle, and other threads spiralling out from the centre. Suspended in the centre of the web was a boy wrapped from neck to toe in the same white material.

The screams had stopped and the boy had his head lowered in exhaustion. When he saw Annie he started to struggle again.

'Hey you,' he said, 'you have to help me! I'm Prince Roger of Rockfield, and I'll reward you handsomely.'

'Of course,' said Annie, and started studying the web to figure out a way to get him down.

Roger did not look happy.

'What are you doing just standing there?' he said. 'Run and fetch a hero or someone useful. The spider could be back any minute!'

Annie sighed and while continuing to study the web she replied, 'Unfortunately, there are no heroes available, and even if there were, by the time I fetched one and brought him back, you would probably already have been eaten.'

Roger went pale. 'Then I shall probably die. It's not as if *you* can rescue me.' He sighed. 'Eaten by a spider, what an unattractive way to die.'

Annie decided to ignore this. If she had been spun up into a web by a giant spider, she would probably not have had the best of manners either.

Roger was stuck to the very middle of the web, high above Annie's head and far from the trees on either side. Annie was sure that if she tried to climb up to him she would end up just as stuck as he was.

The top of the web was secured by three very thick strands wound around the trees. If she could manage to cut those, then the web should fall backwards and he would be low enough for her to cut him free.

'I just need something to cut with,' she said to herself. Her little belt knife, while perfectly good for slicing bread, was definitely not up to the job.

'What?' said Roger. 'What do you want to cut?'

Annie explained her plan and his face brightened up.

'I dropped a sword when the spider carried me up here. It's just at the base of the web.'

Annie fetched his sword from the ground, being careful not to touch the web. It was a very fine sword, with silver wire on the handle and a large red ruby in the centre. She did not have time to admire it though, so she wound Chestnut's reins around a tree-branch, told Squire to stay, secured the sword in her belt, kicked off her shoes and began to climb the tree.

Annie had always enjoyed climbing trees, even though it wasn't really an appropriate hobby for a soon-to-be damsel. This tree had lots of handy bumps and hollows for her hands and feet, and Roger called out helpful directions as she climbed, until eventually she reached the top strand of the web. It was as thick as her arm and very strong, and it took a long time to cut.

'Please hurry,' said Roger, and he looked around nervously.

After a few minutes, Annie realised that a sawing motion back and forth against the web worked best, and eventually the strand broke and the top corner of the web folded backwards. The second strand was easier, and by the time she was halfway through the last one she was humming a little tune to herself.

She was so pleased with herself that she did not hear the spider coming back.

chapter 4

S quire was the first to notice. His ears pricked up and he started to whine worriedly. Annie glanced down to see if he was okay, and then she heard it too.

The forest had become quiet. The birds stopped singing and the little noises that animals make disappeared. Then she heard a chittering noise, and the sound of large legs manoeuvring through the trees.

'It's coming!' shrieked Roger.

'I know,' said Annie, and redoubled her efforts to saw through the web. Finally, it snapped, and the web bent over so that Roger was hanging upside down.

Annie hurried down the tree as fast as she could, but the chittering noise was getting louder and louder. She slipped and fell, scraping her arms until she found a branch to cling onto and then climbed more slowly. When she finally reached the bottom, she dropped the sword and hurried around to the back of the tree where Roger was hanging upside down. His face was red and his breathing was heavy.

Annie took out her belt knife and began to cut away at the webbing material. Once his hands and arms were free, Roger began to help by tearing at the web as she cut it. Finally, with one last cut and tear, Roger tumbled to the ground at her feet.

He stood up and offered her his hand. 'Very nice to meet you,' he said. 'Isn't this just a marvellous ball?' Then his eyes rolled back in his head and he fell over.

The chittering sound was now so loud that Chestnut was whinnying in fear. Annie took out her water bottle and emptied it over Roger's head. He woke with a splutter, and Annie helped him to his feet and ran back to Chestnut and Squire.

'Let's go!' she said, leading the animals towards the road, but Roger was back at the web. He had the sword in its scabbard at his waist, and had picked up a backpack that had been lying in the clearing, but he was searching for something amongst the leaves on the ground. The trees behind the web began to shake.

'Wait,' he called, still searching. Trees and shrubs began to rain down into the clearing, dirt and mud still caking their roots. Something was coming, fast and furious, tearing up the forest in its haste, the thud of falling oak trees mixing with the ever increasing sound of chittering.

'Got it!' Roger grabbed a small box from the forest floor and dashed to meet her at the edge of the clearing. The spider was right behind him.

It was huge, coloured a deep muddy brown and covered in spiky black bristles. It had eight legs, each as wide as Annie's body, leading up to a thick midsection. Towards the back there was a large tear-drop shaped abdomen. Scariest of all was its head, where eight blood red eyes stared at them furiously.

It opened its jaws and gave a harsh roar.

'Run?' said Annie.

'Run,' said Roger.

Heads down, with Chestnut and Squire at their heels, they pushed through the thicket and ran through the trees. The spider was not far behind them. It pushed tree trunks aside with its front legs, and leaped over fallen trunks with its powerful back pair.

Annie looked over her shoulder. It was definitely getting closer, and she knew that it would catch them soon. She wished that she had looked in the book earlier, she was sure her father would have known what to do about giant spiders, but there was no time now.

Then she had an idea. She recognised a fallen tree

in front of them with a funny-shaped mushroom on it. They had definitely come this way before.

She turned left, and Chestnut and Squire followed, but Roger shouted, 'the road is closer this way,' and pointed right.

'I know,' said Annie, 'but I have a plan.'

Roger nodded and followed, too out of breath to say any more.

Then Annie saw the bank of dirt she had been looking for in front of them. She climbed up, wasting precious seconds checking behind her. The spider was almost upon them. She pulled Squire up by his collar, and they all ran forward together. Chestnut remembered the fallen tree from their inward journey and ducked his head.

When they were all safely through, she dropped to the ground exhausted. Roger tried to pull her up, but she pushed him away.

'Wait,' she gasped.

The spider reached the bank of earth, and roared with triumph when it saw them, just yards away.

Its powerful back legs propelled it up to the top of the bank, and under the fallen tree. It opened its jaws, and venom dripped from its fangs as it prepared to catch them at last.

Then it tried to lunge forward, but instead stopped dead. Annie had never considered what a puzzled spider would look like but now she knew. The spider was trapped; the tree-trunk pushing down on its midsection. With its back legs dangling off the bank of earth, there was nothing it could do to get itself free. It was stuck.

Roger yelled in triumph, 'Take that you arrogant arachnid!' he shouted. 'You stupid spider! You ignorant ... insect?

'I suppose it's not really an insect, is it? They have six legs, and spiders have eight,' he muttered to himself.

His face brightened. 'Aha! You ignorant in-vertebrate! They don't have spines you see,' he remarked to Annie, who was looking in the book.

'What are you doing?' he asked.

'Trying to find out how to kill it,' she said.

'Why?' said Roger. 'Let's just get away before it escapes.'

'But then it will just trap someone else,' said Annie. 'I mean, you're a prince, you couldn't just leave a dangerous wild giant spider rampaging around, killing people, spinning webs, ripping up trees ...'

'Yes, of course,' said Roger hurriedly, 'I ... just wasn't thinking.'

Annie went back to reading the book.

Giant Spiders should be avoided at all costs. They are very dangerous, especially to those with magical powers to whom they have a particular attraction. If they must be dealt with, a group of experienced heroes is required to trap them in a large pit.

'Well that advice was a bit late,' Annie thought, and then read the rest of the page.

Once they are trapped they can be killed by plunging a sword into their head where it meets the midsection.

She shared this information with Roger, and looked at him expectantly.

'What?' he said.

'Well, you have the sword,' said Annie.

'Yes …' said Roger, 'but … well … seeing as you were the one who trapped it, you should clearly have the honour of killing it.'

He smiled brightly and handed her his sword. 'No true hero could refuse such an honour.'

Annie wanted to say that she was only a damsel-in-training, not a hero, but somehow she just couldn't find the words.

She took the sword reluctantly and handed Roger the book. She began to climb up the tree, being careful to stay as far away as possible from the hissing spider.

Just as she was about to reach the piece of the

tree-trunk above the spider, Roger called out to her.

'Annie ...' he said.

'Wait a minute,' she said, 'I'm almost done.'

'No, I need to tell you ...'

Annie was balancing on the trunk of the tree with the sword over her head ready to plunge into the spider.

'Shh!' she said, 'I'm trying to concentrate!'

'Annie!' roared Roger, 'Look out for the ...'

Annie brought the sword down sharply and it slid right in between the spider's head and midsection.

'Goo!'

As the spider screamed and slumped down, a fountain of green and brown slime erupted from the wound Annie had made and covered her from head to toe.

'There was a warning on the next page of the book,' said Roger quietly.

chapter 5

They walked in silence until they reached the stream. Annie knew that it wasn't really Roger's fault, but that didn't mean that she wanted to talk to him while she was still covered in spider guts. Roger led Chestnut and carried the book, so that Annie didn't cover them with the foul-smelling spider goo. Squire ran far ahead, wrinkling his nose at the stink and looking at Annie with reproachful eyes, as if she'd done it on purpose!

Roger built a fire and it began to flame immediately, despite the sharp wind. He heated some water while she washed as best as she could in the cold stream. Now that they were not in mortal peril she finally took a good look at him. She had never seen a prince before. The dark curly hair she had noticed earlier topped a freckled face with a strong jaw and cheeks made a ruddy red by sun and wind. The small box he had been searching for under the web turned out to hold a pair of wire-rimmed spectacles that he perched on his nose.

'Bad eyesight,' he muttered when he saw her looking at them, 'my father says it's from reading too many books, but I say there's no such thing.'

Annie gave him a small smile and waited for the water to boil. It was hard to make conversation when you kept being distracted by bits of yourself sticking to other bits. When the water boiled she took the pot behind a bush with her spare shirt and trousers, and washed properly, first herself and then her clothes.

As she spread them out on a rock in front of the fire to dry, Roger took the pot and busied himself making soup.

'Thank you,' she said when he handed her a bowl.

'No, thank you,' said Roger. 'You saved my life, and I got you covered in spider goo!'

'That's okay,' said Annie, 'I'm sure you would have helped me if I'd been the one in trouble.'

'I will,' said Roger.

Annie was confused.

'You saved my life, so now I'm honour bound to help you on your quest. It says so in your book,' he explained.

'Oh,' said Annie, 'wait, how did you know I was on a quest?'

'Well, why else would you be out in the woods when the wizard Greenlott is on the rampage?' asked Roger. 'I wouldn't go anywhere near him if I had a choice.'

Annie supposed that made sense. 'Well, then what quest are you on?' she asked.

Roger gave a rueful little laugh. 'Greenlott put a spell on our castle, so that nobody can enter or

leave. My mother and father and all our knights and heroes are trapped inside.' He sighed wistfully. 'I wouldn't have minded being stuck inside the castle; we have a lovely library.'

Roger began to fiddle with his glasses.

'I know I don't look like much of a hero,' he said, 'but ...'

Roger may not have looked like a hero, but Annie was not even a damsel yet. At least he was a boy *and* a prince.

'Listen,' said Annie, interrupting him, 'I'll let you help me with my quest, but only if you let me help you with yours.'

Roger smiled shyly and offered his hand. 'It's a deal. Two heroes are better than one, after all.'

Annie was again about to explain that she wasn't really a hero, but Roger looked so pleased that she didn't quite know how.

She shook his hand, and he smiled.

'So, what is your quest?' asked Roger.

Annie took another sip of her soup. 'I have to

rescue my father, Tristan Brave, from the wizard Greenlott.'

Roger stared at her. 'You're Tristan Brave's daughter, and I told you to fetch a hero?' He shook his head ruefully, 'What's your plan?'

Annie tapped the book. 'I have his book and it has lots of advice about quests.'

Annie opened her saddlebag and took out the map. 'See, here is the wizard's castle on the Mountain of Misery.'

She took her pencil and put an X on the road just past the troll bridge. 'We're here.'

Roger leaned over her shoulder and bit his lip nervously when he saw the warning about dragons. 'Dragons? I'm not good with dragons …'

'The book will tell us what to do.' Annie shut it confidently.

As Annie drank her soup and warmed herself by the fire she thought about the long road ahead. She had managed to sort everything out so far, but that must have been beginner's luck. She was only going to be a damsel, after all. Roger was a boy, and a prince, and he had a very sparkly sword. She glanced at the poker in her saddlebag and frowned. She should have been relieved to have Roger with her on the quest, but instead she felt a strange kind of emptiness. She had tricked a troll and trapped a giant spider all by herself, and now it didn't really seem to mean anything. She should probably just go home, and let Roger defeat the wizard AND the dragon.

And yet, her father was still missing. He spent his whole life rescuing people and defeating evil, and had written a book so that other heroes could learn to do it better. He'd even talked about starting a school for heroes so that when she needed to be rescued there would be plenty of heroes to help. Now that he needed rescuing, she couldn't just trust someone else to do it. Besides, what if another giant spider captured Roger?

She finished her soup and sighed, 'Oh well, so we've to defeat a ferocious dragon, foil a powerful wizard and travel over dangerous terrain. At least things can't get any worse.'

'Well, there could be a thunderstorm,' said Roger.

Annie laughed and started to gather up her now dry clothes. Then she felt a fat drop of rain fall on her head.

She looked up at the sky and saw dark clouds gathering on the horizon. By the time everything was packed away and they were ready to hit the road they were soaked through. It had come on more suddenly than any other storm Annie had ever seen, and she wondered for a moment if Greenlott had conjured it up.

All thoughts of magic were soon beaten out of her head by the wind and rain. The road was slippery and muddy and Chestnut whinnied with annoyance every time his hoof became stuck. The mud soon reached halfway up Annie's legs.

'We have to find somewhere to shelter!' shouted Roger, but Annie could hardly hear him through the peals of thunder.

'We can't go under the trees when there's lightning!' she shouted back. Roger nodded and they kept on going down the road.

The sky was dark and cloudy, and soon they could hardly see in front of them, except for when flashes of lightning briefly illuminated everything in harsh white light.

Annie was so cold she could barely feel her fingers wrapped around Chestnut's reins. Roger's teeth were chattering and Squire was whining.

'Look!' Roger pointed off the path where a light shone in the distance.

Annie turned towards it quickly. All she cared about was that light meant fire and fire meant warmth. Chestnut whinnied excitedly and began to walk faster, almost trotting.

As they came closer, Annie saw that the light was coming from above the door of a castle of dark grey stone surrounded by a moat. A narrow bridge led across to the thick oak door.

Exhausted, Annie and Roger lifted the huge

brass knocker and banged on the door. Nobody came. Eventually they gave up and turned away.

'Maybe there's a stable or something where we can shelter,' said Roger as they began to cross back over the bridge.

But suddenly, with a great creaking of hinges, the door opened behind them and light spilled onto the bridge.

chapter 6

'What on earth are you doing out on a night like this?'

Inside the door stood a kindly looking lady. She looked about the same age as Annie's mother and was wearing a beautiful blue gown. Her hair was chestnut brown and pinned up in lovely curls.

Looking at her, Annie couldn't help but be ashamed of how awful she must look. Her hair was sodden wet and hung in rat-tails around her face. She was wearing her third-best trousers and shirt, and even her first-best would have caused her mother to throw a fit if she'd worn them in front of anybody. And that was without mentioning the lingering smell of spider guts that even the heavy rain hadn't quite managed to wash away.

But before she could apologise, and even before she or Roger could try to explain why they were there, the lady had swept them across the courtyard. She sent a groom to take care of Chestnut and Squire, and soon had them inside the main castle seated in front of the fire with blankets around their shoulders and mugs of cocoa in their hands.

'Now,' she said, 'I am Lady Anderly.'

'Roger,' said Roger.

'My name is Annie Brave, how very nice to meet you,' said Annie politely.

Before they could say anything else the door opened and a man strode into the room. He was short and stocky, with wide powerful shoulders. He had black hair speckled with silver at the sides and a thin black moustache.

He was wearing a splendid blue waistcoat over a white puffy shirt, and dark blue trousers tucked into black riding boots.

'Darling,' said Lady Anderly as she rose and gave him a kiss on the cheek, 'this is Annie Brave and Roger. They were knocking on our door looking like drowned rats, the poor things.'

'Welcome!' boomed Lord Anderly in a deep rich voice.

He shook Roger's hand and, as Roger winced from the powerful squeeze, he turned to Annie.

'Angelina Brave?' he asked. 'I say, are you Tristan's girl?'

'Well, yes actually.'

'I know your father well,' he said and laughed. 'He said you were growing up to be a fine damsel. Great pair of lungs on you, he said.'

'Thank you,' Annie muttered, avoiding looking at Roger. His mouth was open in shock.

'Isn't this funny?' said Lady Anderly, 'I'm so glad we can help Tristan Brave's little girl.'

Then she frowned. 'But what on earth are you doing so far from home, alone, on a night like this?'

Annie was so tired and Lady Anderly seemed so kind and concerned that she ended up telling her the whole story. How her father was missing, presumed eaten. How her mother had cried. How she had tricked the troll and killed the spider. How she and Roger were on a quest to foil the wizard and avoid the dragon.

'Well, well, well,' said Lady Anderly, 'sounds like you have had quite an adventure.'

She smiled. 'I bet you'd like a long sleep in a comfortable bed.'

'Oh yes please!' said Roger.

'I just hope we are not putting you to a lot of trouble,' said Annie.

'Not at all,' said Lady Anderly, 'we do not have any children of our own, so it's lovely to have you here.'

Lord Anderly took her hand in his. 'It will be nice to have some company.'

Lady Anderly showed them to their rooms, then kissed each of them on the forehead and left them to go to bed. They had been given a suite of rooms in the top west tower of the castle. It had a large sitting-room filled with toys and games. There were huge comfy sofas and a dining-table in the centre of the room. Two large windows with a beautiful view were on either side of a giant roaring fireplace.

Two doors led off this room to lovely bedrooms with huge beds covered in fluffy feather-stuffed comforters. Each bedroom had its own bathroom next door with hot water and all kinds of bubbles and soaps that Annie stared at it in anticipation. She couldn't wait to smell like anything other than spider.

When they were alone, Annie felt Roger looking at her strangely.

'What?' she asked eventually.

'What did Lord Anderly mean when he said you were a damsel?' Roger asked suspiciously.

Annie sighed. 'He meant what he said.'

'You're a damsel?' asked Roger indignantly.

'Yes. At least I will be,' said Annie.

'But I thought you were a hero!' said Roger.

'Well I'm not,' said Annie, 'there were no heroes available.'

'So you're just a girl,' said Roger.

'Just a girl who saved YOU from a giant spider,' snapped Annie. 'I'm going to have a bath.'

She stormed off and filled the bath as hot as she could stand it, tipping in all the bottles so that she was surrounded by walls of coloured scented foam. So what if she was just a girl. She hadn't done too badly so far.

Angry as she was, she felt a flicker of uncertainty in her heart. What if she couldn't rescue her father? What if she just got herself and Roger eaten too?

She worried and worried until she fell asleep. Even then her dreams were troubled as she ran from something enormous and scary while her curls caught in low-lying branches and she tripped over her dress again and again.

The next morning Lord and Lady Anderly woke

them with breakfast in their rooms. They brought bacon, eggs, warm crusty bread, milk, apple juice and a huge variety of jams and preserves. Annie and Roger ate their fill, and Annie thought about how lucky they had been to find such helpful people.

Roger pushed away his plate and sighed with satisfaction. 'Thank you very much for the meal and putting us up for the night,' he said, 'but we should probably get going on our quest.'

'You dear child,' Lady Anderly smiled kindly, 'we can't let you do that. It's far too dangerous a thing for children to do.'

'Perhaps you can go later,' said Lord Anderly, 'until then, you will be very happy here with us.'

Then they opened the door and stepped outside.

'Wait!' said Annie, 'How much later?'

'Oh, not very long,' said Lord Anderly.

'Just five or ten years,' said Lady Anderly.

The she blew them a kiss and closed the door.

Annie and Roger looked at each other in horror as they heard the key turn in the lock.

chapter 7

'Now look what you've gotten us into,' said Roger.

'What *I've* gotten us into?' said Annie. 'You're the one who saw the castle.'

'You're the one who told them all about our quests!' said Roger. 'And you're the one whose father they know.'

'It's not my fault if they know him,' said Annie, 'he's quite famous.'

Then she had an idea. 'Wait! You're a prince. You can just order them to let us go.'

'Oh,' Roger started to fiddle with his glasses. He mumbled something.

'What?' said Annie.

'I'm not actually a prince,' he said quietly.

'But you said you were,' said Annie. 'You said you were Prince Roger of Rockfield, and your mother and father were stuck in the castle!'

'They are stuck in the castle. So are the king and queen. It's just, my father's an armourer and my mother's a chambermaid,' said Roger.

'But, you have a shiny sword,' said Annie.

'I was taking it out to be cleaned, wasn't I?' he said. 'Anyway, *you* said you were a hero.'

'No I didn't!' said Annie. 'You just thought I was a hero, and I didn't say I wasn't. You SAID you were a prince.'

'Well, I didn't think you'd rescue me if you knew I was just a servant boy,' said Roger.

'That's just great,' Annie threw herself down on the sofa, 'you're a servant boy and I'm a damsel in training, and we're stuck in this castle while our parents need rescuing.'

Roger sat down beside her. 'Let's just figure out how to get out of here and we can fight about it later.'

Annie sat up. 'Good plan. Any ideas?'

'No,' said Roger.

'Me either,' said Annie.

It was a very long way down from the window, and even when they knotted all the sheets and towels together, the drop would probably have killed them. The walls of the castle were too smooth to climb and the only door was thick, heavy and very definitely locked.

It was mid-morning by the time they had exhausted all these possibilities, and Annie began to shiver.

'If we're going to be stuck here we may as well be warm,' she said, and began to lay kindling in the fireplace.

Just as she lit the tinder, Roger pushed past her. Annie thought he would be burned, but instead the fire went out as he stepped into the fireplace and stuck his head up the chimney.

'What are you doing?' asked Annie.

Roger poked his head out, covered in soot,

and smiled triumphantly. 'I think I've found a way out.'

'Up the chimney?' asked Annie hesitantly.

'In Rockfield castle I spent a few weeks working as a chimney boy when I was younger,' said Roger. 'They were all connected.'

He disappeared back inside the chimney and a few minutes later called down to Annie.

'Come on up!'

The chimney was dark and sooty, and Annie found it quite difficult to breathe. There were hand and footholds carved in the stone walls, but they were slippery with soot, so it was not an easy climb.

Annie climbed and climbed until she found Roger waiting for her in a passageway that led off left and right from the chimney.

She caught her breath and rubbed the soot out of her eyes.

'Which way?' she whispered.

'We have to find a fireplace that's empty and close to the stables,' answered Roger.

Annie tried to remember where their tower was in relation to the courtyard. She pointed right and Roger nodded.

The passageway was only just big enough for them to crawl through on their hands and knees, and there was soot everywhere. Annie almost felt sorry for Roger as he followed her and had to breathe in all the soot that she kicked up. But he was a liar and deserved it.

It took half an hour of crawling before they found another chimney. It was narrower than the one in their room but looked just wide enough for them to pass. Annie gingerly leaned out from the passageway and when she did not feel any heat, slowly began to climb down.

They climbed and climbed, and Annie felt herself begin to slip many times before managing to keep her handholds. She began to feel like the chimney was closing in on her. Then she realised it was. The chimney had gradually been getting narrower, and now it was pushing against her hips.

'Roger!' she squealed. 'I'm stuck!'

'What?' said Roger and, startled, he let go of his handhold and fell right onto Annie. The impact dislodged her and they both fell down the chimney. Annie was convinced that they were going to die, but they only fell a few feet before reaching the fireplace and collapsing in a heap.

Annie groaned, and opened her eyes to see a startled groom looking back at her.

'Aaagh!' he said.

'Aaagh!' said Annie.

'Ow,' said Roger.

'You're not supposed to be out of the tower,' said the groom. Then he took off running out the door.

'Wait!' said Annie, but it was too late. He had gone.

Annie and Roger followed him, and found themselves in a large stable.

'Chestnut!' called Annie, and was rewarded with a faint whinny from the end of the barn.

Chestnut and Squire were in a stall at the end of the stables. They looked happy and well fed, and Chestnut nibbled Annie's hair companionably as she bridled and saddled him.

Annie scrambled up into the saddle and pulled Roger up behind her.

'Squire! Heel!' she called, and kicked Chestnut into a canter. They barrelled out the open stable door and into the courtyard. Chestnut wheeled and headed for the castle gate, but Lord and Lady Anderly were already there.

Lady Anderly smiled. 'How very resourceful of you to escape from the tower,' she said, 'but we have already removed the bridge.'

chapter 3

Lady Anderly was telling the truth. Beyond her, outside the open gate, Annie could see the flickering of sunlight on water.

'Now that you have seen for yourselves that you cannot get away, won't you come in for some nice lunch?' asked Lord Anderly.

Annie's shoulders slumped; they were trapped. But her father was missing, and there was nobody else to find him.

'Hold tight,' she whispered.

'What are you going to do?' asked Roger, but he tightened his arms around her waist all the same.

Annie kicked Chestnut into a gallop and headed straight for the gate, Squire running beside them.

Lord and Lady Anderly leaped out of the way and Roger held on for dear life as Chestnut's muscles bunched underneath them. Annie closed her eyes and hoped.

Then she felt a jolt as Chestnut landed on the far side of the moat. He scrambled up the bank and Annie turned him back towards the castle as Squire swam across the water.

'Thank you for your hospitality,' she called. 'But we have quests to finish and a wizard to defeat.'

'You are only children!' called Lady Anderly.

'This is a job for heroes,' shouted Lord Anderly.

'Yes,' said Roger, 'but we'll just have to do.'

Annie kicked Chestnut to a canter and they headed back to the road.

They travelled all day, eating lunch on the road. Annie and Roger had cheese sandwiches from their packs and Chestnut had his nosebag full of oats. Squire made do with some of the tongue that Annie had packed. Their only stop along the way

came when they met up with the Western River and took the opportunity to wash off some of the chimney-soot and fill up their water-bottles. Even then, they didn't speak.

When night fell they camped at a clearing close to the Western River. They were all exhausted and built their fire and made their camp without speaking. The silence was only broken when Squire began to bark furiously down by the river.

Annie and Roger went to investigate and found Squire standing guard over a patch of reeds in the shallows.

'Yuck,' said Roger, 'a frog.'

The frog's back leg was tangled up some reeds, and it was struggling helplessly.

Annie told Squire to sit, and began to untangle the reeds.

'Father says you should always be nice to frogs, in case they're a prince under a magic spell,' she said. 'We had to train Squire not to eat them. That would be an awkward thing to explain to a king.'

When the frog was untangled, she sat him on her hand and gave him a kiss.

The frog sat there solemnly. 'Ribbit,' he said, and then jumped into the river.

Annie washed her hands in the water and wiped her lips with a handkerchief.

'No luck there,' she said.

'Yuuurgh,' said Roger. 'I'm glad I'll never be a damsel.'

'Well I'm glad I'm not you! At least I'm going to be a something. You're just a servant boy. You're a nothing!' said Annie, and she stormed off down the river.

Annie regretted it almost instantly. It was not Roger's fault that he wasn't a prince, any more than it was her fault that she was not a hero. The difference was, Roger could still become a prince. Her father had told her all the stories when she was little. He could rescue a princess, or defeat a giant, or even be a prince already and just not know it yet. There were no stories about girls becoming heroes.

Girls were always damsels until they were rescued. They were captured, rescued, married, and that was it, whereas a hero could go on heroing for as long as he liked, or at least until he was eaten.

She sulked in the woods until she was tired, and then she went back to camp. Roger was already tucked up, fast asleep.

'I'll apologise to him in the morning,' she thought.

As she fell asleep, a pair of watery eyes watched her from the river. When she was fast asleep, another pair joined them, and then another, until soon the whole river seemed to be made up of cold, still eyes.

chapter 9

Perhaps if Annie had not been so tired from the adventures of the day, she would have woken up during the night. If she had, she would have seen the stars moving above her head and heard the lapping of the river against her sleeping bag. She would have seen that she was being carried, sleeping bag and all, down the river.

She would have looked down to see what was carrying her and perhaps recognised the frog she had rescued earlier. She might not have though, as he was only one small frog among the hundreds who supported her on their backs as they swam.

After some hours, she would have seen the small frogs replaced by larger ones, and the larger ones replaced by huge ones, until she ended up safely deposited on an enormous lily pad in a circular pool.

However, Annie was very tired, so she did not wake, and she did not see any of these things. Instead, she woke up as the morning sun shone in her eyes, and found herself on the lily pad in the pool.

At first Annie thought she was still asleep and dreaming, so she simply looked around curiously.

The pool was surrounded by high rocks on either side. They seemed both natural and unnatural, as if there had been a framework of rocks off the river, and someone (or something) had dragged others over, and dug out a channel to create this wide, still pool.

Seated on lily pads all around her were enormous frogs, as big as Squire, with lustrous shining skin. They ranged from a pale bluish green, to a deep oak-leaf colour. The largest frog was sitting on a lily pad right in front of her. He was almost as tall as she was, and three times as wide, and his skin was bright emerald, fading to grass green on his enormous belly. He was wearing a lily flower crown and held a heavy gold sceptre. He had a wide lipless mouth and a huge yellow pimple just above his left eye.

'What an odd dream,' thought Annie. Then she realised that she could feel the dampness of her sleeping bag and the chill in the air. She could smell the musty mouldy odour of the frogs, and she was suddenly very certain that this was not a dream at all.

She tried to sit up, but she was tied to the lily pad with slimy strings of pond-weed.

'Hello my darling,' croaked the frog, 'I'm glad that you have woken up.'

'Who are you?' asked Annie, 'what am I doing here?'

'I am Hertzog,' said the frog, 'and I brought you

here to thank you for saving one of my subjects.' He pointed with one long slimy finger at a little frog floating in the water.

Annie relaxed a little. 'Well, you're very welcome,' she said, 'but I must get back to my camp.'

'Ribbit, Ribbit, Ribbit!' laughed Hertzog, and the other frogs laughed with him until the whole pool echoed with froggy laughter.

'Quiet!' roared Hertzog, and his cheeks inflated and grew red with rage. The laughter stopped instantly. His cheeks deflated slowly. 'Words are a poor thank you,' he said, 'I must do something more.'

'That's perfectly all right,' said Annie nervously.

'No it isn't!' screamed Hertzog.

He croaked imperiously and some smaller frogs paddled over with a large lily pad on which was set a table. The tablecloth was made of pond-weed and algae, the cups were empty eggshells, and there was no cutlery to be seen.

The servant frogs sat Annie up in a bulrush

chair and loosened her hands enough for her to eat, but not, she quickly found, enough to escape. Hertzog sat himself down opposite her.

'Music!' he croaked, and four frogs began to croak rhythmically.

'Drinks!'

Their cups were filled with a brown liquid that looked exactly like watery mud. Annie sniffed it and discovered that it also smelled like watery mud, and decided that she would not risk a taste.

'Food!'

Annie was a little bit hungry, but her hunger soon disappeared when they were served. A large fat greyish frog brought her a leaf covered with wriggling brown bugs and slimy fat worms. She recoiled in disgust.

'Eat!' shouted Hertzog, muffled by the large quantity of bugs he was pulling into his mouth with his tongue.

'Or is there something wrong with the food I have prepared?' he asked menacingly.

Annie watched as a bug crawled out of his mouth and made a dash for freedom up his face.

'No!' she said, 'It's just ... I'm ... watching my figure.'

The bug had made it to the top of his head. 'Most commendable,' said Hertzog. With a snap, his tongue grabbed the bug and dragged it towards his mouth.

Annie flinched.

'So, my dear. My little friend here says that after you rescued him, you kissed him. Is this true?'

'Well, yes,' said Annie.

The frogs began to ribbit excitedly, but when Hertzog's cheeks started to inflate they quietened quickly.

'Excellent,' he croaked, 'then you are indeed worthy.'

His voice rose and he raised his arms to the assembled frogs. 'My frogs! Meet your new princess!'

The croaking became a roar.

'No!' shouted Annie, 'You don't understand!'

The croaking stopped instantaneously.

'No?' said Hertzog, 'No!? How dare you say "No"!'

'I'm very flattered,' said Annie, 'it's just, I only kissed him because I thought he might be a frog prince.'

'Well I am a Prince Frog,' said Hertzog, 'which amounts to the same thing. So we shall be married.' He grinned horribly, his long sticky tongue rolling out of his mouth, 'You are nearly a damsel, and I have rescued you, so I get your hand in marriage and half your father's kingdom.'

Hertzog raised an eyebrow, causing his pimple to bulge. 'Does your father have a kingdom?'

'No,' said Annie, 'but ...'

'No matter,' Hertzog waved his hand magnanimously.

'You didn't even rescue me from anything!' said Annie, getting more and more panicked.

'But I did. Are you not a young girl, out in the world with only a boy for protection?'

'Well yes, but …'

Hertzog leaped onto the adjoining lily pad and again raised his arms. 'My frogs! She has accepted my proposal!'

'No I didn't!' said Annie, but she could not be heard above the croaking of the frogs.

They picked up her chair and spun it around and around and around until she was dizzy. Some of the frogs began to croak a celebratory song, and still others came up to pat Hertzog on the back and shake his webbed hand.

'I WILL NOT MARRY THAT FROG!' shouted Annie.

The frogs fell silent, and dropped her chair onto a lily pad with a splash. They looked in terror at Hertzog as his cheeks inflated and grew ruby red.

'Is that your final word on the matter?' he croaked menacingly.

'Yes,' said Annie, 'yes it is.'

'Very well,' he said, 'if you won't marry me, then you shall never marry ANYONE!' and with that he raised his sceptre high in the air and brought it straight down towards Annie's head.

chapter 10

As the sceptre came towards Annie's head and she imagined it smashing into her skull, the heavy gold weight ending her life, time seemed to slow down. She saw her father, trapped by the wizard, calling for her. She saw her mother weeping by the fireside for her lost husband, and now her lost daughter too. She saw her little brother Joffrey growing up without a big sister to protect him. She saw Roger, Chestnut and Squire waking up to find her gone, and not knowing where she was or what had happened to her. Then she saw a sword. It darted in between her head and the sceptre, and she felt the rush of air as it narrowly missed her nose and heard a crash as gold met steel.

Roger pushed Hertzog back with his sword, and the frog leaped to safety on a nearby lily pad. They began to circle each other, jumping from leaf to leaf. The other frogs croaked in alarm and some of the larger ones moved closer to the fight.

'Do not worry,' croaked Hertzog, 'I will deal with this impudent boy.'

The frogs moved back to the walls of the pool, and watched the contest eagerly.

Annie felt a cold slimy touch on her hand and shuddered.

'Get away from me, frog,' she hissed, but then smiled when she looked down. Squire gave her another quick lick as he doggy-paddled in the water before returning to the task of tearing at her bonds with his teeth.

As Squire loosened her ties, Roger and Hertzog continued to fight. Hertzog was on the attack, using his long sticky tongue to distract Roger and upset his footing while he tried to get close enough to connect with his sword.

Annie wriggled out of the slimy pond-weed ties and stood up, looking around wildly for a weapon. Squire scrambled up onto the lily pad and whined in frustration when she grabbed his collar. He let out a sharp bark and Roger glanced over. In this moment of distraction Hertzog took his chance. His long sticky tongue wrapped around the hilt of Roger's sword and sent it flying, and his long legs kicked out at Roger's ankles.

He stood over Roger, smiling horribly.

'So this boy is why you will not marry me?' he said, and raised his sceptre.

'Wait!' screamed Annie.

Hertzog paused with the sceptre held above his head and Roger at his feet.

'Perhaps,' croaked Hertzog, 'if you ask very nicely, I will let you have his life as a wedding present.'

Annie looked down at her feet for a moment, and then stared Hertzog right in the eye.

'I suppose there's only one thing I can say.'

She let go of Squire's collar.

'Go get him boy!'

Squire leaped straight across the pool and landed with his heavy front paws on Hertzog's chest. The frog toppled over, croaking wildly as he lost his grip on the sceptre.

The watching frogs shrieked in panic, and some began to jump into the water.

'Stay back or the dog eats him!' shouted Roger, scrambling to his feet and retrieving his sword from the next lily pad. He pulled Squire away and held Hertzog captive until Annie made her way across to them and bound Hertzog's hands with slimy pond-weed.

They made a strange little procession out of the pool: Hertzog at the front followed by Roger with the sword, then Annie, then Squire, and the rear brought up by a panicking, croaking crowd of frogs.

Chestnut was waiting for them outside. Annie motioned for the crowd of frogs to stay back as they mounted, and Squire guarded Hertzog.

'Kill me with the sword rather than the dog,' croaked Hertzog and his cheeks puffed up nobly.

'I'm not going to kill you at all,' said Roger, 'but I am going to charge you not to kidnap any more potential fiancées, and if I've heard you have, I won't come back here.'

Hertzog perked up.

'I'll send the dog and his friends.'

Hertzog's cheeks deflated. 'It's not my fault I'm a frog,' he said sadly.

'It's not because you're a frog,' said Annie, 'it's because you are a horrible creature. You could have been the most handsome, human, wealthy prince and I still would not have married you. You're a bully and a tyrant and that's why nobody will marry you.'

With that, they cantered off.

When they were safely away from the river they stopped and made a fire to dry themselves out a little.

'Oh Roger,' said Annie, and gave him a hug, 'however did you know where I was?'

'Squire woke me up in the night, whining,' he said, 'and you were not there. So I packed up all our things and followed Squire down the river bank. When I found the pool that awful frog was about to clobber you, and next thing I knew I was fighting him. I didn't even think.'

'I worried that maybe you would think I had just left,' said Annie.

Roger began to fiddle with his glasses. 'I did for a minute, but then I figured you wouldn't have left Squire and Chestnut behind, no matter how angry you were with me.'

'I'm not angry any more,' said Annie, 'it's not your fault that I'm only going to be a damsel. And I'm sorry for what I said before. You may not be a prince, but you are definitely a hero. Just look at how you saved me back there.'

Roger looked at her oddly. 'Well, you saved me from the spider, so doesn't that make me a damsel and you a hero?'

Annie sighed. He just didn't understand.

'Anyway,' said Roger, 'I think Squire rescued both of us back there.' He scratched Squire behind the ears.

'Hey!' said Annie, 'what's that he has in his mouth?'

Squire spat it out obediently. It was the frog's sceptre.

Roger picked it up, 'I wonder if it's worth anything?' he asked. Then he shrugged and threw it for Squire to fetch. They doused their fire and continued on down the road.

'Where are we now?' asked Roger, as they rounded a bend in the road. 'Did the frogs take us very far out of the way?'

Annie did not answer. Straight in front of them, towering up to the sky and wreathed in clouds, was the Mountain of Misery and, at the peak, a plume of smoke marked the wizard's castle.

chapter 11

'ight,' said Roger. 'Now we just have to get past the dragon.'

'And then infiltrate the castle of the most fearsome wizard in the land, find and rescue my father, defeat the wizard to rescue your parents, and get all the way back down the mountain and past the dragon again,' added Annie.

'I was trying not to think about that,' muttered Roger.

Roger took her hand and they walked silently along the winding trail through the foothills and into the mountain forest.

'Maybe we will not even see the dragon. Maybe she is busy. Or napping. Or off terrorising somewhere else. Maybe the map's wrong and she does not live here any more. I don't see any dragon signs, do you?' Roger looked around hopefully.

But the stillness of the sky was disturbed as the dragon launched herself into the heavens. The sun reflected and sparkled brighter still off her scales, gold and green against the blue. She soared high on the updrafts, chasing her tail on the winds and circling the mountain before diving back into the forest.

She reminded Annie of a fire. Beautiful but deadly, and one could not be separated from the other. And though she loved fires, she would have doused them all to bring her father home safe.

'I guess not,' Roger sighed glumly.

'We had better move to the side of the path under the trees, so she can't see us from the air.' Annie led Chestnut under the branches as she spoke, and Roger followed.

There were no sounds in the forest, not even the rustlings of deer and birds. Occasionally they came upon blackened circles where trees had been charred and uprooted. The ground was covered with ash and as they passed through, their feet and Squire's paws and Chestnut's hooves kicked it up and filled the air with grey clouds that made them cough and splutter.

'It's as bad as Castle Anderly's chimneys,' said Annie.

'Not quite, we haven't fallen yet,' said Roger. As he spoke, his foot became tangled in a tree-root half hidden by ash, and he fell on his face. Annie did not laugh, she was too worried about the dragon and the wizard and their impossible task. A girl, a servant boy, a horse and a dog, trying to succeed in a hero's task. It was a fool's errand, but she could see no other way than forward.

By nightfall they were halfway to their destination and the trees were beginning to thin out, with brush and scrub filling in the ground-cover.

'Best to make camp here where there's still cover,' said Roger.

'You're right,' said Annie, and she led Chestnut over to one of the few unburned trees, tying his reins to one of its leafy green branches.

Annie fetched water while Roger lit the fire, their camp routine familiar at this stage. As the fire burned low Annie sat cross-legged in front of it and opened the book.

'What does it say about dragons?' Roger leaned over her shoulder.

'I don't know, I haven't read that far yet.' Annie ran her finger down the index to the entry marked **dragons** and turned the pages to its place.

'Annie ... it's blank!' Roger's breath came fast and his voice was strained.

'I can see that,' she snapped and turned the pages. Ten sheets left aside for dragons and not a single word marred the perfection of the parchment.

'It must be somewhere else! Give it here!' Roger grabbed the book from her, his hands shaking as her own fell listlessly to her sides.

'He said it wasn't finished ...'

Roger began to breathe deeply. 'It's okay. Maybe there's another way to the castle. Maybe we can just avoid the dragon.'

Annie pulled out the map and spread it out on the ground, tracing their route with her finger.

'There's only one way.'

'There has to be another way!' Roger's voice cracked.

There was no other way, but there was no way back for Annie. She could not go home without her father, not having come so far. She crawled into her sleeping bag as Roger frantically flicked through the book.

'What're we going to do Annie?'

She closed her eyes and thought of her father.

a hero is a man who continues to try, even when all hope seems gone.

She was not a man, but she could still try. 'We do our best,' she replied.

As she drifted in to sleep she clung to one comfort – at least she was not alone.

But when she woke up in the morning, Roger was gone.

She knew before she opened her eyes. She could not hear the little sounds he made in his sleep, but it was more than that. The camp felt different, empty, abandoned. Deserted. Betrayed.

She rose from her bed and began to pack up the camp, cinching Chestnut's saddlebags closed as he nuzzled her hair. Squire sat in Roger's empty place, his paws resting on the sword and book placed carefully beside the fire. The sword weighed down a clean piece of parchment torn from the book.

Written on the parchment in a fine, skilled hand was: *You are more worthy of this than me. R.*

Annie crumpled it in her fist and tossed it on the fire. She slid the sword into her belt and packed the book before scrambling into Chestnut's saddle and heading up the trail.

Squire whined and remained sitting at the fire, glancing anxiously around the camp.

'He's not coming back, boy. We're on our own. C'mon.'

Squire trailed behind, looking back over his shoulder every few minutes. Annie envied him his ignorance, that he could simply miss a friend without knowing why he had gone, that he could face the road ahead without fear.

'I will try,' she told herself, and pushed her fears away, concentrating on the path and the sound of Chestnut's hoof-steps.

What had seemed foolish when Roger was with them seemed like madness now. Face a dragon, defeat a wizard and find her father, all on her own. Well, with Chestnut and Squire, but while she could talk to them they couldn't offer her comforting words, or advice, or even just worry with her so that she felt less alone.

The path grew narrower while the cliffs grew steeper, winding between grey stone slabs that leaned in overhead, blocking out all but a narrow slit of sky and casting the path in shadow. Annie could hear her own breathing echoing off the sides, and the clip-clop of Chestnut's hooves bouncing through the passageway, resonating and reverberating so that it seemed like there was an army with her.

She wished she had an army so she could lead them right up to the dragon and cut off its head, then storm the castle and beat the wizard until he cried out for mercy. But there was only herself.

She heard the sounds of battle later than she should have, only when the path left the cliffs behind and continued through the forest. It had been drowned out by the echoes of the mountain passage, but she heard it soon enough to jump down and lead Chestnut off the trail and into the brush. She crawled forward though a beech thicket until she could see the source of the noise.

The dragon stood proud and tall in front of a dark cave, her body as tall as Annie's house and

twice as long. Her scales shone brighter than sunlight on clear water, dazzling and distracting. Her wings were fully spread, muting the sunlight that passed through them, dappling the clearing in green and gold. Her long sinuous neck supported a finely carved head that wove back and forth in agitation.

Annie's mouth was dry with fear. She couldn't move, though all she wanted to do was run away, run home to her mother and her brother and hide under the bed and wait for someone else to bring her father home. But there was no one else, not even Roger, and her mother would be crying. She couldn't run, but how could she fight a dragon?

A knight stood before the dragon, his horse whinnying in panic and straining at her tether, which was tied to an oak at the edge of the clearing. His armour shone almost half as brightly as the dragon's scales, and he did not seem afraid.

'Your reign of terror is over, monster!'

'My reign of terror? What exactly is it I've done?'
The dragon spoke in a voice like the crackling of
tinder, harsh and musical all at once.

'I won't play your games, foul beast.'

The knight spat on the ground in disgust.

'Prepare to die, Piperazine!'

He shouted a war cry and ran forward, sword
raised above his head.

The dragon roared and the clearing filled with
shining whiteness. The flames burned with the
pure deadly brightness that can only come from
dragon fire. Annie closed her eyes but the scene
was imprinted on her mind; the knight, tall and
proud with his sword raised high, and the dragon
on her haunches, wings spread wide above them.

When she opened her eyes all that was left of the
knight was red hot armour glowing on the ground
and a skittish grey mare neighing in panic. As she
blinked the scene from her eyes, red-hot tears
running down her face from the scalding light,
Annie became aware of a hand on her shoulder.

chapter 12

nnie almost screamed, but bit her lip to stop herself. She whirled around with the sword in her hand only to pull back mid-thrust and almost over-balance.

'Roger?' she whispered, mindful of the dragon, but also hardly wanting to speak in case he was a figment of her imagination.

His black curls fell over his forehead and onto his spectacles, but underneath his eyes shone with fear and determination.

'I'm sorry.'

'That's okay, I understand.'

He bit his lip. 'I left, like the coward I am. I don't know how I can make up for it ...'

'You made up for it by coming back.' Annie smiled and threw her arms around her friend.

'You may as well come out,' said Piperazine. 'I suppose I could flame you where you stand, but I always like to see my prey.'

They pulled away and looked at each other in horror.

Piperazine laughed, a sound like the crackling of green wood as it burned. 'I can smell your fear sharper than a well-charred stag.' The fire raged. 'Show yourselves!'

Roger and Annie had no choice but to push their way through the brush, and though Annie told them to stay, Chestnut and Squire followed, so that soon they were all standing at the edge of the dragon's clearing.

As close as they were now, she was even harder to look at. Her scales shone and sparkled like a thousand jewels had been inlaid on her skin, but their brightness was not the reason they looked away. Her green eyes were flecked with gold, utterly inhuman and filled with the promise of death.

Piperazine drew in a breath and purred, 'Any last words?'

Annie desperately tried to think of something, anything to say. She was frozen with fear and her mind was blank.

'Actually,' said Roger, 'there is one thing. How do you keep your scales so shiny?'

The dragon looked as surprised as it is possible for a dragon to look. 'These old things?'

'Don't be modest,' Roger chided. 'They're the most beautiful sight I've ever seen.'

Piperazine flowed down onto her stomach and rested her head on her forelegs. 'You really think so? It's disgraceful how the younger dragons don't bother to keep up appearances. A healthy scale is the sign of a healthy dragon, that's what I always say. It's why I keep to a strict diet of wild-caught game, nicely charred, with charcoal once a week. Only beech charcoal of course.'

'Of course.' Roger sat down on the ground companionably. 'But that can't be it. You must have a special secret.'

The dragon looked around conspiratorially. 'Well ... don't tell anyone, but when I want to look really impressive I give them a good rub-down with olives.'

'That's genius!' Roger clapped his hands in excitement. 'Tell me, have you ever thought of using pine resin?'

'Pine resin?' The dragon nibbled at a talon thoughtfully.

'I think it would give a lovely sheen.'

The dragon tilted her head. 'You know, I think you might be right ...'

Annie could not keep her mouth shut any longer.

'Did you say you only eat wild-caught game?'

Roger and Piperazine looked at her as if their fascinating conversation had caused them to entirely forget her existence.

'Well of course,' said Piperazine, 'this figure doesn't keep itself.'

'It's just, we thought you were on a rampage. Stealing cows, eating people ...'

Piperazine began to make odd little noises and coughed thick black smoke out of her nostrils and Annie realised she was trying not to be sick.

'I? Eat people? Euugh! Have you any idea how many parasites you humans carry? Euugh! And you're all salty and tough, and I have to pick clothes out of my teeth and euugh!'

'I'm sorry,' muttered Annie, 'but I saw you flame that knight.'

'Flaming people?' Piperazine shook her head. 'I flame people all the time, but that is because they come at me with swords. I certainly do not eat them afterwards. I wish they'd stop bothering me, it's a terrible waste of fuel.'

'But they're only coming because they think you eat people,' said Roger. 'Have you told them about your diet?'

'I never get a chance to! They just come rushing in shouting "avast evil beast" or "die foul fiend" and then I flame them and it's too late.' She sighed sadly and curled her tail around herself, shaking her head.

'We could tell them for you,' offered Annie.

'Would you?' Piperazine sat up brightly. 'I would be ever so grateful, and you can take that knight's horse with you. I've no need for it.'

'No problem,' said Annie and swallowed nervously, 'but … before we go, could you tell me if you recall flaming a hero by the name of Tristan Brave?'

'Tristan … Tristan …' Piperazine twirled her tail thoughtfully.

'He's very tall and has curly blonde hair like mine, but shorter.'

Annie tried not to choke on her fear.

Piperazine shook her head. 'I don't recall the name, but I flame an awful lot of people …' she shrugged her shoulders. 'Well, if he was here,

I flamed him. None of them have ever gotten away.'

'Thank you,' said Annie and bit her lip so that she would not cry. She gathered Chestnut's reins and put her hand on Squire's collar, drawing comfort from the warmth of his fur. Her father was dead, burned up in an instant, in white-hot dragon fire.

Roger calmed the grey mare and led her around the edge of the clearing. Together they headed towards the trail.

'He could have taken the other path, I suppose,' said Piperazine thoughtfully.

Annie jerked around and Chestnut harrumphed, almost pulled off balance.

'Other path?'

Piperazine began to sharpen her claws on a rock. 'There is a path to the wizard's castle that does not go by my cave. I have seen a lot of heroes going up that way and none of them have ever come back to bother me. I'm quite grateful to that wizard Greenlott.'

chapter 13

annie could hardly contain herself. 'There's another path? My father could have taken another way?'

'Oh no Roger, we *have* to go past the dragon,' muttered Roger. 'There's *definitely* no other way, Roger. Worst map ever.'

Annie could barely even scowl at him, she was so excited. Her father might still be alive.

'We have to go to the wizard's castle.'

Piperazine pointed to the path up the mountain. 'Not that way you won't. There was a rockfall a couple of weeks ago. Well, more of a rock-push. I thought if the path was blocked maybe less heroes would come by me on their way to the wizard's castle.' She peered down her nose at them.

'Obviously that is not the case.' She nibbled on her talon again. 'Maybe I should make a sign ...'

'We'll go on the other path then,' said Annie.

Piperazine shook her head and twiddled her talons. 'You'd have to go all the way down the mountain again, it would be very inconvenient, and I suppose if you're going to make sure nobody bothers me any more I do owe you a favour.' She nodded her head decisively. 'I shall just have to carry you over the blockage.'

'Carry us?' Annie swallowed nervously. Piperazine had seemed to fly very high and very fast when they had seen her earlier.

'Carry us!' Roger whooped with glee.

The dragon cocked her head. 'It may be wise to blindfold your horses and block up their noses if possible. They tend not to appreciate my perfume.'

Annie secretly agreed with the horses. Piperazine smelt like wood-smoke and a well-oiled sword, silver and gold, blood and tears, all underpinned by a sharp acrid scent that screamed dragon. But the fastest way to anywhere was by dragon-flight, that or walk through shadows, for which she would have needed unicorn's tears.

The misty grey horse was already pawing nervously at the ground, tugging at Roger so hard that he was almost lifted off his feet. Chestnut was behaving, but his ears were back and his muscles tense. She glanced at Roger and shrugged.

'I'll get blindfolds!' He started searching through his saddlebags – exceedingly difficult when the saddle is attached to a nervous grey mare who keeps trying to back out of the clearing.

Annie headed out of the clearing and into the woods towards the mountain pass. She had smelled something before, something she recognised. She closed her eyes and breathed deeply, in through her nose. There! She stumbled forward, then to the right, then into a tree. She rubbed the bump on her forehead and headed left, until the scent filled the world around her and she opened her eyes.

She was in a thicket of wild-growing mint. Woody stems and broad leaves surrounded her in a maelstrom of brown and green and there was an overwhelming scent of freshness and life.

There was a tangle of it outside her bedroom wall. Her father had brought home a seedling once, and it had grown, spread and flourished until in a few short years it reached halfway along the house. Her mother had wanted it cut back because it was untidy and wild, but her father had always put it off. 'It's life!' he would say, then pick a leaf and crush it between his fingers, releasing the scent and laughing.

Annie blinked back tears and began to harvest leaves to make nose-blocks for the horses. Her father could still be alive, and if he was, she would find him and bring him home.

When she had enough, four good handfuls and extra for luck, she hurried back to the others. On the way she heard a scream. She dashed into the clearing, ready to grab the sword and stab the dragon if she could, then started laughing so hard that she fell on her knees. The grey mare was running around in circles in a section of clearing blocked off by Piperazine's body and tail, with Squire guarding the exit. Roger's legs were tangled in the reins so he was hanging upside-down, one hand clinging onto the saddle so that he was not dragged along the ground.

'Help please!' he gasped.

It took Annie longer than it should have to catch the mare, as every time she got close and saw Roger's expression, with his face all red from exertion and blood flowing to his head, she started to laugh again and the mare would get away. Eventually, she caught the reins and disentangled Roger while apologising for her mirth.

'It was pretty funny, I suppose,' said Roger. 'Anyway, we're going to be riding on a dragon!'

'I'd managed to forget about that,' sighed Annie.

'Hurry up, hurry up!' said Piperazine. 'I don't have all day: places to be, things to flame.'

'Yes ma'am.'

Roger hurried around to the horses and blindfolded them, while Annie wadded up the mint leaves and pushed them into their noses. They did not like it very much, but it was better than having them kick and scream while hundreds of feet up in the air.

Annie mounted up and she pulled while Roger pushed to get Squire up on Chestnut's back and then into her lap. Once Roger was on the grey mare Piperazine spread her wings and launched herself into the sky. They watched her as she climbed high into the air.

'Do you think she's forgotten us?' asked Roger, just before Piperazine swooped down, faster than a hawk, and scooped them up with her front talons.

'Nope!' said Annie with a shriek as the ground dropped away and they flew through the sky.

chapter 14

In a matter of minutes, they had covered as much ground as they had the whole previous day on foot. The ground below them looked like a painting, trees as small as blades of grass and the track like a little brown snake winding through the trees and cliffs. Piperazine set them down on the track some way from the wizard's castle.

'I don't really want to get involved with the wizard. He has been very good with keeping heroes away from me. But do remember to tell them I'm not eating people!' With these parting words she was gone, a sparkle in the sky.

'That was amazing!' Roger hopped down and took off the mare's blindfold as well as fishing the mint out of her nose. She whinnied in annoyance and wiggled her nostrils, but once she looked around and saw that the dragon was gone she began to buck and prance like a foal.

Annie slid off Chestnut and threw up noisily in the bushes.

'I don't really think dragon-flight is for me.'

The rest of their journey up the mountain went much faster than before they had met Piperazine. With two horses, they moved at a speedier pace, and the horses were eager to leave the dragon as far behind them as possible, despite her strict dietary requirements. The grey mare gradually calmed as they covered ground and Roger patted her neck and whispered in her ear as he rode.

The trail grew narrower as they ascended, winding through high cliffs and clinging tight to the edge of narrow gorges.

'I think I shall call her Mistful,' said Roger. 'She's a misty grey and she seems kind of wistful, so if you put the two words together you get Mistful.'

The mare snickered and nibbled at some leaves from a low-lying branch.

'See! She likes it!' he said, patting her, 'don't you, Mistful.'

Annie nodded absently, lost in thought, half-formed plans, and a terrible fear that she would never find her father.

'And Mistful and I shall be best friends for ever and ever, and when I'm old and grey our hair will match and everyone will be terribly impressed and … you kind of hate me don't you.'

'Yes, definitely,' she said. 'Wait, what?'

The words tumbled from Roger's mouth as he fiddled with his spectacles with shaking hands that still held reins. 'I left, and I'm awful, and I'm dreadful, and I'm such a coward. You must hate me; I hate me quite a lot right now.' He almost fell off the horse, and a brief interlude while he grabbed Mistful's mane and righted his balance gave Annie time to think.

'I don't hate you. I did for a little while, but it

wasn't your quest.' She brought Chestnut to a halt where the track became too narrow to ride and slid to the ground. Roger joined her. 'I'm just glad you came back. You're my friend.'

Roger settled his spectacles back on the bridge of his nose and nodded his head decisively. 'Excellent. We shall be friends for ever and ever as well.' He frowned. 'I don't think you would look particularly fetching with grey hair though, we shall have to dye it a kind of auburn colour to match Chestnut.'

Annie was not listening. At the end of the trail, flags flying dark against the sky, was the wizard's castle.

Annie stared up at it for a moment before pulling Roger off the road and pushing him face down into the scrub at the side.

'What was that for?' asked Roger, spitting grass out of his mouth.

'Ssshh!' said Annie, and mashed his face back into the mud.

'Seriously, I'm getting annoyed now,' grumbled Roger. He pushed her off him and rolled onto his back, still grumbling. He shut up very quickly when he saw the castle through the bushes.

Annie took the book from her saddlebag and turned to the page marked **wizards**.

Wizards may be good or evil. Obviously, the good kind are the best kind to meet. They can provide you with magic swords, everlasting sandwiches and healing potions. However, even good wizards should not be annoyed. They can be very tetchy and may turn you into a frog.

Evil wizards are the worst kind of wizard to meet. Their powers can be very extensive. They may be able to create whole buildings, turn people into animals and animals into people, and brew compulsion spells and killing potions.

Annie swallowed nervously. She hoped her father had not been given a killing potion.

To defeat an evil wizard is very difficult. There are only two ways. They can be killed by use of their own magic against them or by removing their amulet and either destroying it or giving it to another wizard. It is better not to destroy the amulet as they are very valuable and can be used by good wizards to set damage right.

'Read about amulets,' said Roger.

Annie turned the page.

Amulets are used by wizards to focus their power. Once they have been used for a lot of spells they have a hold over the wizard's power. They may be made of any kind of stone. They glow when touched with gold and are best destroyed with fire.

'Right,' said Roger, 'so we get in, find the amulet, break the amulet, defeat the wizard and leave.' He paused, 'But we'll need something gold to find out what the amulet is.'

Just at that moment Squire dropped the Prince

Frog's sceptre at their feet and looked at them hopefully.

'We can't play fetch right now,' said Roger.

'Squire, you genius!' said Annie, hugging the dog. 'The amulet will glow when we touch it with this. Who'd have thought that frog would turn out to be helpful?'

'The only problem now is getting in,' said Roger.

They sat in the brush for a half an hour, thinking.

'What about … No,' said Annie.

'Or maybe … Nah,' said Roger.

'This is getting ridiculous!' said Annie, and she marched out into the road.

'What are you doing?' hissed Roger, following her.

'I'm going to walk down there, knock on his door, and see if he wants a servant,' said Annie, 'what's the worst that could happen?'

'He could turn you into a frog or a goat or give

you a killing potion or put a compulsion spell on you,' said Roger.

'Look!' snapped Annie, 'my father could be in there, about to be chopped up, or eaten, or turned into things. I am NOT going to waste any more time on prince frogs or protective lords and ladies or flirting with dragons or sitting around doing nothing.'

Roger sighed. 'Well then at least let me catch up.'

The wizard's castle was black and green, with high pointed turrets topped with dark flags. It towered over the landscape. Even though it was far smaller than the mountain behind it, the castle seemed larger. It was a man-made structure, but seemed more real than the mountain borne naturally from the earth.

The door was aged oak, stained mossy green. A heavy, black, cast-iron hammer hung as a handle in its centre, just above Annie's head. She swallowed nervously, her courage drained by the imposing castle, then steeled herself and lifted the heavy black hammer.

Knock ... Knock ... Knock ... The sound echoed far more than it should have. Furious barking erupted from inside the castle and Squire flattened his ears back against his head.

The door creaked open and a fearsome deep voice shouted, 'who dares to disturb the great Wizard Greenlott!'

'Annie and Roger,' said Annie hesitantly, 'we wondered if you were looking for servants.'

The wizard stalked towards the door from the shadows inside the castle. He was short and thin. He had curly brown hair tied up in a pony-tail and he wore velvety green robes.

'Servants?' he said, and began to laugh with a high manic cackle. Then, as suddenly as he had started, he stopped when he reached the doorway. He looked quizzically at Roger.

'Why yes,' he said, 'I could do with some servants. Come in.'

They hitched the horses to the door and followed him inside. The hall was covered with dogs. Big dogs, little dogs, brown dogs, white dogs, curly-haired dogs and straight-haired dogs. Squire sniffed at them curiously and whined, butting his head against Annie's hand.

Greenlott ignored the dogs and hurried up the stairs. He stopped outside two doors and tucked a necklace back inside his shirt. It had a silver chain attached by four silver points to a huge emerald, at least as big as Annie's hand. Annie elbowed Roger excitedly.

'You can have these two rooms,' said Greenlott abruptly.

'Thank you,' said Annie.

'What duties would you like us to perform?' asked Roger.

'Any victims or prisoners you want fed or tortured or anything?' asked Annie hopefully.

'Prisoners?' Greenlott began to laugh. 'I keep no prisoners. I have battled over fifty heroes and won every fight, and I have no cells. Even Charles the Chivalrous and Tristan the Brave could not defeat me.'

He pointed at Roger. 'You can ... mend things, I suppose, and feed the dogs. You,' he pointed at Annie, 'can feed the horses and sweep the floors.'

He then swept back down the stairs, the children forgotten behind him.

Annie slumped to the floor and rested her head in her hands. She had failed. Roger crouched down beside her.

'Who's to say he's even telling the truth, Annie? This castle's huge – there are plenty of places that cells could be hidden.'

Annie nodded, dried her eyes and allowed herself to hope.

Over the next few days, Annie became more and more certain that the wizard's amulet was his necklace. He wore it all the time and hastily tucked it back into his shirt whenever it fell out. Despite this breakthrough, Annie became more and more disheartened.

She searched the whole of the castle, bringing a sweeping brush with her in case Greenlott asked her what she was doing. She had plenty of time to search, as the floors did not seem to get dirty, simply absorbing any dust that fell on them. Greenlott did not bother her. He spent his time closeted in his laboratory, making potions and casting spells. He often called Roger in to help him, and at first Annie thought he would want her also, but he never called her.

She was a little bit insulted, but at least it gave her more time to search. She looked everywhere, from the attics to the cellars, in all of the towers and the stables, and behind every door, but there were no prisoners. At last, she had to admit what she had feared most.

Her father was not there.

chapter 15

She spent the whole night crying. She had failed. She should never have come. She was only a girl, and the wizard had defeated fifty heroes, her father one of them. Now he was gone, and she did not think she could even be a proper damsel any more, because after this journey, she was not sure if she could ever wait to be rescued like she was supposed to and not try to help herself first. She had not wanted to admit it to herself, but she had started to secretly hope that if she rescued her father he would see that she could be heroic herself. Perhaps she could have persuaded him to teach her to be a hero instead of having to marry whatever man rescued her like tradition dictated. She thought of Hertzog and shivered. But her father was not here. Some hero she was.

The next morning she dried her eyes and found her courage again. Roger's parents were still held captive and she had promised to help him.

She found him in the stables, feeding the horses.

'Roger, we have to get that amulet.'

'Yes, but Greenlott wants me to come up to his workshop. He cast a spell yesterday and today he is going to teach me how!' said Roger excitedly. 'He has such wonderful books.'

Annie was furious. 'Have you forgotten why we're here? He killed my father and trapped your parents.'

Roger started to fiddle with his glasses, 'Yes, of course, but ...'

'But nothing! How are we going to get his amulet?'

'He takes a nap every day at three o'clock,' Roger muttered.

'Right,' said Annie, 'let's test the emerald then. Make sure to bring the Prince Frog's gold sceptre.'

Roger nodded and they parted ways.

Annie waited all morning. She fed apples to the horses and swept floors that were not dirty, and tried not to think about her father. She did not see Roger for the rest of the morning. One of the wizard's dogs had taken a particular liking to her. He was a yellow curly-haired dog, with deep brown eyes and a wet brown nose and he had started following her from the moment she stepped into the castle. She had thought that Squire might be a bit jealous, but he seemed to love this dog, always licking him and playing with him and staring at him.

She had swept everywhere that could be swept, even though there was nothing to sweep, so she sat with the dogs on the balcony and leaned her brush against an emerald statue. 'What shall we do while we wait for Roger?' she asked them. Of course they were dogs and could not answer.

'You could look at what's right in front of your face,' said a voice from behind them.

Annie bit back a scream and wheeled around. There was nobody there.

'Who said that?'

'Who do you think?' said the statue. 'Not very bright, are you?'

Annie pursed her lips. 'Well I'm not going to stand around here and be insulted by a statue.'

'Going to go find that boy, are you?' asked the statue. 'Oh, let me guess, he's busy, isn't he? I wouldn't rely on him if I were you.'

'What do you mean?' asked Annie.

'He's left you before, hasn't he?' The statue smirked.

'Shut up!' said Annie, 'that was different.'

'Oh it was,' said the statue, 'he didn't have anything else then, he did not have a world of magic and power opened up to him. But he still left you. This time it *is* different, and he won't come back.'

'Shut up!' shouted Annie. 'What do you know? You're just a statue. You can't even move!'

'I can listen,' said the statue, 'and I can watch, and I have not heard or seen anything that would make me think he cares about you at all. Oh, and I can think, which is more than I can say about you. Such a stupid little girl.'

'Shut up!' screamed Annie and she grabbed her brush and hit the statue so hard that the head came right off. It rolled along the floor and came to a stop against her shoe.

'Temper, temper,' it said. 'Don't you know you can't kill a magic statue by hitting it? So stupid.'

It began to laugh and Annie kicked it into the corner and ran out to the stables. Roger would not betray her, she was sure. Well, mostly sure. He had left her before, that was true, but he had come back. And he did seem happy here with the wizard, but surely he still wanted to help his family? She paced nervously around the stables while the yellow dog whined in the corner.

When three o'clock came around, she tiptoed up to Greenlott's room, and found Roger waiting outside. She breathed a sigh of relief. What did that statue know, anyway.

'Do you have the sceptre?' she whispered.

'Yes but ...' Roger began to fiddle with his glasses. 'Greenlott was going to let me do a spell this afternoon, so I thought maybe we could wait until tomorrow.'

Tears began to form in Annie's eyes. 'Roger, don't you want to help your parents? Don't you want to help my father's memory? Don't you care about what this man's done?'

'Of course I do,' muttered Roger, 'it's just ...'

'Just nothing!' hissed Annie and pushed open the door to Greenlott's room.

Greenlott was fast asleep in front of a huge fire, the flames burning eerie and green, feeding not off wood, but off the wizard's magic. His emerald necklace was hanging out of his shirt. They quietly made their way over. Roger took the Prince Frog's sceptre out of his pocket and touched it to the emerald. It began to glow. Annie caught her breath. It was the amulet. She carefully lifted the chain over Greenlott's neck and tucked the amulet into her bagful of apples. Her fingers pressed against a small bump on the silver and the emerald fell away from the chain and mingled with the green apples.

She stepped back and froze as a floorboard creaked. Greenlott opened his eyes, looked at her, and then down at his chest, to where the amulet should have been.

She ran, but Greenlott was faster, and he grabbed her around the throat, his long nails digging in so hard they almost drew blood. She grabbed the chain from her bag and quickly pressed the silver points into an apple before throwing it to Roger.

'Boy, give me the emerald,' Greenlott said menacingly.

'Why?' asked Roger. 'You'll kill us once you have it.'

'Kill you,' Greenlott laughed, 'I would not kill

you, my boy. I want to teach you. Why do you think I took you into this castle in the first place? Wizards have no need for servants.'

The wizard smiled and extended his hand. 'You have power in you, boy. Power that I can unlock. Just give me the emerald and I can make all your dreams come true. I can make you strong.'

'You're lying,' said Roger.

'Haven't you always felt special, Roger?' asked the wizard. 'Haven't you always found that strange things happen around you? A certain knack for lighting fires, perhaps? A strange talent for changing the weather? You cast that spell yesterday, Roger, not I. You can be more than a simple servant boy.'

Annie gasped: suddenly what happened with the fire in Anderly Castle, the suddenness of the storm and the spider's attraction to Roger started to make sense.

Roger held the silver chain and twirled it, as if considering this. Annie held her breath.

'What about Annie?'

Greenlott shrugged. 'What about her? She is just a potential damsel. You can keep her if you want.'

'I *don't* want to be a servant boy,' Roger said slowly.

Greenlott smiled and held out his hand.

'I want to be a hero.'

Roger threw the chain into the fire. Greenlott screamed and jumped in after it, and Annie twisted away. But before he could reach it Greenlott was caught by his own magical fire. First flames appeared on his hair, fingers and toes. They spread upwards and inwards until he was totally covered in flames.

Annie and Roger stood transfixed as the wizard burned. Then Annie felt the floor begin to shake. Green flames began to appear on the walls and the ceiling.

'Run?' said Annie.

'Run,' said Roger.

As they ran, the building began to collapse around them, but instead of burning and turning

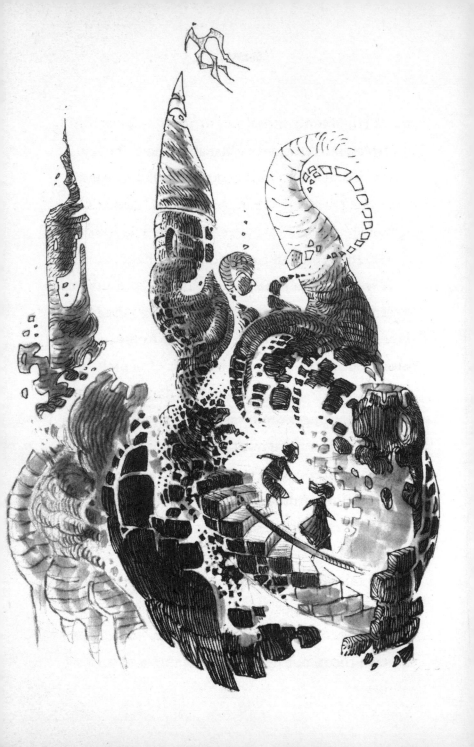

to ash, the wood and stone of the castle rapidly disappeared as the flames touched them.

'It's the magic,' said Roger, 'as Greenlott burns everything he created with his magic is unmade.'

Annie nodded, and leaped across a hole that opened up in the floor below her.

They made their way across rooms and down stairs, hopping from stone to stone as they vanished, sliding down banisters that disappeared as they passed.

Once on the ground floor they dashed to the stables. Roger released the dogs and Annie the horses. The horses whinnied in fear as walls fell apart and ceilings came crashing down, only to disappear before impact.

At last, they were all outside, safely away from the walls of the castle. Soon there was nothing left but a small pile of sticks and stones.

'Well done Roger!' Annie hugged him.

He hugged her back, 'I told you he didn't want servants,' he said.

Annie thumped him and Roger laughed, then sighed. 'I wish I hadn't had to destroy the jewel,' he said sadly. 'Not that I would have sacrificed you for it,' he added quickly.

Annie took the emerald out of her pocket and pressed it into his hand.

'But how?' gasped Roger.

'I swopped it with an apple.'

Roger laughed, then sagged a little at the knees. 'Oh dear,' he said.

'What?' said Annie. Had he been hurt? Was the wizard still alive? Was there a monster nearby?

'What on earth are we going to do with all these animals? I wish they were a bit more manageable.'

Then something very peculiar happened. As Roger was talking, some of the animals rose up in the air and were covered by a thick green smoke. The smoke billowed around and around faster and faster, until suddenly, it was gone, and so were the animals. In their place were men, some with beards, some with moustaches and some clean-shaven. Some had long hair, some had short hair and some had no hair at all. Despite these differences, the men all had something in common. They were all heroes. And there, in the middle of them, was Annie's father.

'Father!' she shouted, and ran to him. He picked her up in his arms and spun her around before putting her down abruptly.

'Angelina!' he said. 'What on earth are you doing here? It's very dangerous. I have been captured by the Wizard Greenlott and ...' he looked around confusedly.

'Where is the wizard? And where is the castle? And what are all of you doing here?'

'Last I remember, he was turning me into a guard-dog,' said one hero.

'He said I would be a horse,' said another.

'Moo ...' said a third, and then coughed apologetically.

'But we could only have been released from

this enchantment if Greenlott was defeated,' said Annie's father.

'It wasn't me,' said a grey-haired hero.

'Or me,' said a hero with a big black beard.

Soon all the heroes had chimed in, and none of them knew who had destroyed the wizard.

Then Annie's father saw Roger, standing aside looking a little embarrassed. 'I say, young man,' he said, 'I am Tristan Brave, hero at large. Who are you and what do you have there?'

'My name is Roger,' he said, 'and this is Greenlott's emerald.'

'Did you defeat Greenlott?' asked Tristan.

'Technically, yes,' said Roger, 'But Annie ...'

'Is that the sceptre of the Prince Frog?' interrupted Tristan.

'Yes!' said Roger, 'Annie ...'

Before he could finish he was interrupted by impressed mutterings from the crowd.

'Very impressive!' said Tristan, 'I suppose you've bested a dragon and killed a giant spider too?'

The heroes laughed.

'Well, yes actually,' said Roger, 'but Annie ...'

Whatever he was saying was drowned out by the heroes. They began to chant 'Roger! Roger! Roger!' and picked him up on their shoulders while Annie stood, lonely and forgotten, to one side.

chapter 16

They took the other track down the mountain, so as not to bother Piperazine. Roger eventually managed to get Annie alone while she was washing at the river. She had been avoiding him, spending time with Chestnut and Squire, or else with her father and his heroing friends. She did not like to spend too much time with them though. Charles the Chivalrous kept making everyone stand up whenever she came to the logs they were using for tables, and again when she left, even if she was just going for a second. One night she had helped put away the dishes and he had made everyone stand up ten times in fifteen minutes.

John the Giant had ridden away on the first day and not come back for hours. Everyone was worried he had been eaten by wolves or attacked by dwarves, but he caught up with them later with a big smile on his face and a dress in his hands for Annie.

'I bought it off a farmer with a little girl your age. It must have been awful not to be able to wear your nice, pretty, normal clothes,' he said kindly.

Annie was quite comfortable in her raggedy trousers and coat, but he had seemed so pleased with himself that she couldn't disappoint him, so she put on the dress, even though it was hard to keep clean and meant she had to ride Chestnut side-saddle.

She was down at the river trying to get mud off the hem of the dress when Roger finally found her.

'Oh Annie,' he said, 'I'm so sorry. Every time I try to tell them how heroic you were they start cheering me and singing ballads.'

'That's all right,' said Annie. 'I don't care anyway. I'm not ever going to be a hero.'

She walked off back to camp. She didn't care, really. She was happy for Roger and all the attention he was getting. She was going to be a damsel and there was nothing wrong with that. It was just that she would have liked to have a choice.

And actually, it wasn't fair. Everyone just assumed she had been tagging along with Roger, having been lost or something. He had saved her a few times, but she had saved him too, and now he was getting all the credit.

The heroes were weary and hunting for food for so many was difficult, so after two days of hard travelling they stopped at Anderly Castle. Annie managed to avoid Roger until their first meal in the dining hall. Lord and Lady Anderly hugged her and petted her head and told her she had been very lucky to have Roger along to protect her. She gritted her teeth and smiled and managed not to jab out their eyes with rusty spoons. They were very excited to have so many guests, and they added to the mighty tales of Roger with his (not theirs, HIS) daring escape from the castle.

Their minstrel even wrote Roger a ballad and performed it at dinner. Annie blocked her ears with pieces of bread, but it didn't work.

Then Roger stood up on the table.

'Hurrah for Roger!' called one of the heroes, and the others took it up, until all that could be heard throughout the hall was 'Hurrah! Hurrah! Hurrah!' Annie wished Roger would wait until she finished her dinner. She just wanted to eat her meal in peace.

'Quiet!' said Roger, 'I have something I'd like to say.'

The heroes hushed, and listened respectfully.

'Thank you very much for the ballad, it's beautiful. But ...' he began to fiddle with his glasses, 'there are some errors in it.'

He took a deep breath. 'I did not kill the spider. I did not single-handedly defeat the Prince Frog. I didn't stand alone against Greenlott or Piperazine and I certainly wasn't always brave and strong in the face of danger.'

The heroes looked puzzled.

'But we saw the sceptre!' called one.

'How are we free if the wizard was not defeated?' asked another.

Roger took his glasses and set them firmly back on his nose.

'The spider was killed and Piperazine befriended. Hertzog was humbled and Greenlott was defeated. That much is true. I was there for the adventures, and I had some hand in them. But I was not alone. I had a companion, brave and true, and while sometimes I saved her, she saved me as much or more. Any mighty deeds or heroic feats you want to praise me for, you must praise her too. Annie Brave is as much of a hero as I am.'

With that, he stepped down off the table and hurried out of the hall, leaving everyone staring at Annie.

'Angelina, is that true?' asked her father.

'Kind of … mostly … yes,' she said.

'Well I never!' said Randolph the Thin.

'Girls rescuing people?' snorted John the Giant.

'I certainly wouldn't allow MY daughter,' sniffed Charles the Chivalrous.

Annie's father looked at her very oddly indeed, but before he could open his mouth she got up from the table and fled.

She found Roger in the stables, brushing down Mistful as Squire and Chestnut looked on.

'I'm so sorry,' he said, 'I just couldn't take all the credit for your bravery and …'

A flying tackle of a hug interrupted him.

'Oh Roger,' said Annie, 'shut up. I'm proud of you for being so brave,' she swallowed a sob, 'and I'm going to try and be brave as well.'

She got up and dusted off her knees. 'I had better find my father,' she said.

'Good luck,' said Roger.

Her father was not in his room. Annie laid a fire

in the grate and sat in front of it. After some time her father came in, brushing straw off his boots.

Annie had practised a speech in the empty room. How she loved him, and did not want to disappoint him. How she only wanted to make him proud. How she could not simply sit back as a damsel and let herself be rescued when she was sure she could do it herself. But all her fine words left her and she found that all she could do was speak from the heart.

'Father, I don't want to be a damsel. I want … I want …'

Roger had stood up in front of all the heroes. Surely she could speak to her own father.

She took a deep breath. 'I want to be a hero. I want to help people, like you do.'

He barely looked at her before sitting down at his desk and scribbling in his book. She sat back down in front of the fire and tried to hold back her tears. The fire was reduced to embers when she finally heard a creak as her father sat back.

'I've finally finished it,' he said cheerfully. '**how to slay dragons - and other advice for the hero in training** by Tristan Brave. It's finally complete.'

'Well done,' said Annie, and poked a particularly glowing coal with a stick.

'Would you like to hear the dedication?' he asked.

'Sure,' she said. She wondered if she could split the ember in two.

'To my darling wife,' he said, 'my wonderful son, and my beautiful daughter, who will be an astounding damsel someday. Unless ...'

Annie sighed, and then realised what he had said. 'Unless what?' she asked.

'Unless she becomes an even better hero,' he said.

Annie turned and saw him smiling at her, his eyes filled with pride, and before she knew it she had crossed the floor and was hugging him tight.

'That Roger boy is quite remarkable,' he said, 'he will be an excellent pupil in my new school for heroes.'

He hugged her close and whispered in her ear, 'and so will you.'

the end

acknowledgements

A full list of acknowledgements would be more words than are in my book, but I would like to briefly thank those integral to this book and my general mental health whilst writing, revising and waiting for publication with bated breath. My agent Faith O'Grady and all at Lisa Richards, who thought they were signing a schoolteacher and were confronted with a student.

My editor, Eoin Purcell, who clearly didn't know what he was letting himself in for when we met up for drinks. Everyone at Mercier for their dedication and support. Axel Rator for the beautiful pictures. Sarah and Sinéad, my S-club writing buddies, for word choices and cupcakes.

All at the Cherry-Bomb and Death-Trap for giving over their living room. My drinks and dinner buddies; Ruth, Elizabeth, Mary, Jarvey, Gregg and Ross (both Kelly and McGuire) for keeping me sane. The L&H for the public speaking skills and friends for life. The staff and students of UCD Vet – especially Barry, Carolynne and Kat. The *University Observer* in UCD for giving me a start, Nathalie, for being the first to say I deserved to be paid for my writing, and Nadine O'Regan for the free books. The Debs of 2009, a classy bunch of awesome. My family, for the roof over my head and the seventeen bookshelves. And Shane, just because.

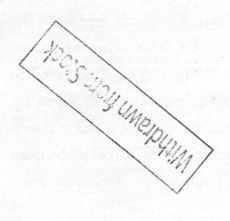